Don't Be Afraid

It's Just One Of Pop-Pops Stories

Dennis Corcoran

Don't Be Afraid
Copyright © 2024 by Dennis Corcoran

ISBN: 978-1962497596 (sc)
ISBN: 978-1962497602 (e)

The Reading Glass Books
(888) 420-3050
www.readingglassbooks.com
fulfillment@readingglassbooks.com

Table of Contents

1. Hermit On The Hill

It was here, 50 years ago today...The house your Grandparents lived in. They had just been married, and recently returned from their honeymoon. They settled down one evening in their cozy new home, nestled in the woods, surrounded by towering Oak trees and thick pine trees. Back then, the road was quiet and dark.

Every now and then a car would pass by. During the light of day, as your Grandparents, worked in the garden that faced the street, they would wave as a car passed by. It didn't matter who it was, they figured they must know them. It was a small town, several miles from the nearest village where they could shop for food, go to church and get gas for their car. They never met him, but the Hermit on The Hill often passed by in his old beat up pickup truck, and they waved.

That evening, the sun had set, and there was a full moon peeking through the trees. It was a crisp Autumn night, and your Grandparents were watching TV. The flames from a warm fire were flickering in the stone fireplace. They were feeling thes magic of their new life together.

Unexpectedly, there was a screeching sound from outside that seemed to drag on forever, followed by a sudden and loud shriek of crashing metal. Then there was silence.

They looked at each other and jumped to their feet. Looking out the front window, and with the light of the moon, they saw shadows of a pickup truck, wrapped around the big Oak tree that stood majestically at the edge of the road in front of their home. They knew they must run out to see what happened. Maybe they shouldn't have. As they approached the pickup truck, mangled and destroyed, they feared what they might see next.

Willy was a lonely man that lived by himself, deep in the woods, up on a hill a couple of miles from the house. He lived in a shack with no electricity or running water. The townspeople knew him as the Hermit On The Hill. Willie drove his old beat up pickup truck that had survived way beyond its normal years, never stopping to say hi to anyone. But he knew your Grandparents would wave to him as he passed by. Willie's face matched his truck, wrinkled and worn beyond his 50 years.

Your Grandparents were horrified as they approached the wreckage, realizing that what was wrapped around the tree was the pickup truck from the Hermit On The Hill. The carcass of a deer with a trail of blood laid still on the side of the road. They proceeded cautiously to the mangled destruction, Grandma following Grandpa. Broken glass covered the road, and the smell of burnt rubber filled the air. But what Grandpa saw next stunned him in a way he would never forget.

The hermit on the hill was slumped back, leaning against the driver's seat. His eyes were wide open, staring up at Grandpa. Before he could turn his head away, a raspy voice declared, "Thank you for waving to me. I'll be back next year to celebrate my birthday".

Grandpa went back to the house to call the police. When the police arrived, there was no-one in the car. The Hermit On The Hill had disappeared. The carcass of the dear remained with a trail of blood, but what happened to the Hermit on the Hill?

No-one knows. Every year on his birthday, the nightmare returns. The sound of screeching tires and crashing metal fills the air. The moon is always full, and the leaves from the shaken Oak tree fall to the ground. The voice from the Hermit on the Hill is unmistakable, echoing into the night. "Thank you for waving to me. I'll be back next year to celebrate my birthday."

Don't be afraid. You know it's just Pop-Pop, telling his stories. But the Hermit on the hill might be back next year. If you see him, just wave, and wish him Happy Birthday.

2. Don't Go Into The Tunnel

The two brothers loved adventure, and they loved trains. So one day they decided to hike down the old train tracks to the train tunnel. They walked all morning, and finally reached the tunnel. Jack walked up to the edge of the dark tunnel and couldn't help but think of what might be back there. The concrete platform next to the track was raised up from the tracks with weeds growing out of the cracks. Jack warned his brother Luke to be careful not to fall over the edge. The train tracks below the platform were barely visible, covered by dirt and debris from years of neglect. If anyone fell into the tracks, it would be hard to get out.

Jack and Luke couldn't resist venturing into the darkness of the tunnel. Luke remembered that he had a little flashlight in his pocket that Pop-Pop had given to him. He always kept it in his pocket, because he loved shining it in peoples faces. Of course that annoyed people, but Luke just laughed when they told him to stop. But now, Luke wanted to point his flashlight into the tunnel to see what might be back there. So he pointed it into the darkness of the tunnel.

The tunnel was so old and dark that they could not see much, but soon they heard a voice. The voice got louder, and then a shadowy figure came into their sight.

Jack and Luke were frightened by the voice, and hesitated to go further. They waited in suspense to see who was walking out of the darkness. Luke kept the flashlight on, and Jack called out " Who's there?".

They fought the urge to run back to the light at the end of the tunnel, and finally a shadowy figure came into view. Luke kept his flashlight pointed toward the approaching man.. As he approached, Jack and Luke saw horror on the man's face. He was breathing heavily, and could barely get the words out. But gasping for breath, he yelled out, "Don't go back there"!

Jack asked, "Why"? Luke was shining the flashlight in his face. The man said, "get that light out of my face"! Luke lowered the flashlight.

The man started to describe what happened to him and his friend in the tunnel. "We were walking into the tunnel to get to the other side.. Before we got too far we heard an unmistakable sound. It was a train horn, and it was getting louder and louder. Then we saw a light. The light got brighter, and the horn got louder. It was pitch black, and we were blinded by the light of the train. What happened next, I can't explain".

The man told Jack and Luke that the train was racing down the track, out of control. They thought it was going to crash. Just before the train was about to reach them, they jumped over to get as close to the wall as they could to avoid the train. There was a thunderous crash. The train then disappeared down into a hole. The platform they were standing on cracked into pieces. The man's friend lost his footing and slipped into the dark hole.

The train was gone. His friend was gone. Jack and Luke didn't know what to do. They wanted to go further into the tunnel to see what happened. The man said to them, "Don't go back there. There's a hole that ate up the train and my friend."

The train and the man's friend were never found. They say the hole is still there. It goes to the center of the earth, where things simply burn up.

But Don't be afraid. This is just another story from Pop-Pop. Just Don't go wandering into any train tunnels. You never know what you might find.

3. Antler Man

Many years ago, something very strange happened in the woods behind the house. A hunter shot a deer, but left the carcass in the woods. The only thing the hunter took was the antlers from the male deer.

The kids in the neighborhood had a tree fort in the woods, near where the hunter had shot the deer. It was their place to play after school. They would get off the school bus, rush home to finish their homework and venture into the woods to climb up to the tree fort, where they could tell jokes and laugh with no adults around.

One day, one of the boys was standing on the roof of the tree fort looking out into the woods. The others heard him shout, "There's a dead deer, let's go check it out!".

They all climbed down the tree fort latter and ran over to the lifeless remains of the deer that had settled in a pool of dried blood. One of the boys said to the others, "he has two holes in his head". One of the other boys thought out loud, "That must have been where his antlers were!'.

As soon as he said that, something happened that frightened all of them. A man came running out of the surrounding trees holding the deer's antlers above his head, like they were his own. As quickly as he appeared, he disappeared back into the woods.

The boys were startled with what had happened. They did not go back to the tree fort. Instead, they ran home, fearful of what they had seen.

That night, each of them went to bed, thinking about the man with the antlers. Where did he come from? Why did he cut the deer's antlers off, and why did he run past them holding the antlers above his head.

As they lay awake in their beds, hoping to fall asleep, they each heard a tapping sound on their windows. It was like someone had a stick, banging it against the glass. They all had the same reaction. When they looked at the window... It was the man with the antlers, tapping the deer antlers against the window. They each ran to their parents to tell them what happened.

Of course, when their parents came to the bedroom and looked out the window, there was no sign of the Antler Man. They all said the same thing. "That's just your imagination".

The boys knew it wasn't just their imagination. They knew it was the Antler Man. They saw him with their own eyes. They lay awake each night waiting to hear the antlers tapping on the glass, and waiting to see Antler Man's face peering through the window..

Years passed, and the Antler man became a legend.

Every now and then, kids in the neighborhood say they hear tapping on the window. They see a man with antlers peering through the glass. Their parents say the same thing, "It's just your imagination".

So if you ever hear tapping on your window at night Don't look, you might see Antler Man. Maybe it's your imagination, maybe not. But Don't be afraid, Pop-Pop loves to tell this story.

4. What's Under the Ice?

The lake froze up each year in the winter time. In the coldest months, the ice was thick enough to hold the weight of an ice house. The ice house was a tiny little shack with no floor. Fishermen hauled the ice shack out onto the lake so they had a warm place to sit while fishing. They drilled holes in the ice, dropped their fishing lines, told stories and laughed while they waited to catch fish.

One year, four boys that lived around the lake and played together everyday thought it would be fun to go out to one of the ice shacks at night. They made a plan to sneak out of their house and meet down by the lake.

That night, they each laid awake, waiting until they were sure their parents were asleep. Then, they snuck out to meet at the lake. It was cold and dark, but they all dressed in warm clothes with gloves and heavy boots.

The moonlight sparkled off the shiny ice. They could see the shadows of a nearby ice shack. They made their way toward the shack, trusting the thick ice to hold their weight, walking carefully so they didn't slip.

When they got to the shack, they had to duck their heads to get through the short doorway. They sat on the benches that were placed on each wall, facing each other. It was cold, and they could see each other's breath as they talked. They began to relax, laughing and telling jokes. Their boots reached the solid ice below the bench. In the middle of the ice floor, water trickled over the surface where the fishermen had cut holes to drop the fishing lines.

One of the boys said, "We should have brought some fishing line and bait so we could catch some fish"! Another one said, "The fish are probably asleep now". As soon as he said that, water from the fishing hole shot up, splashing freezing cold water onto their hands and face. "What the heck was that", one boy said. The others just looked at the hole in the ice, not knowing what to say. The water settled, but they couldn't stop looking at the hole in the ice. One of the boys finally spoke. "Maybe we should go". They all looked at each other, wondering what to do. Another boy spoke up. "I agree, I think we should go back".

They all decided to leave the ice house, and lined up at the doorway to head back. Just before the last boy was getting to the open door, they heard a scream. They turned back to look at what was happening, and couldn't believe what they were seeing.

It looked like a snake, but it was larger than an alligator. Its mouth was opened wide with two big fangs and a long pink tongue. The creature grabbed their friend's legs with his fangs, and began to swallow the boy. His gloves slipped off, and his hands were stretched out, as he grasped at the slippery ice. His face looked horrified as he screamed for help.

The three other boys grabbed his arms, struggling with all their might to stop him from getting swallowed up. The creature was pulling all of them toward the fishing hole, continuing to swallow the boy. The ice was slippery, and the other boys couldn't stop the creature from pulling them toward the hole that was now large enough for them to fall through.

One by one, each of the boys had to let go. They watched their friend get swallowed up by the creature as it slithered back into the water. The last thing they saw was their friend's hands grasping at the slippery ice, and then he disappeared.

The boys all had the same reaction, and ran back to the shoreline. They slipped and fell, desperately trying to run across the ice to get help. But it was too late. Once the boys returned with their parents to the ice shack, all they could see was a big hole in the ice.

The boy was never found. Only his gloves remained, frozen into the ice on the floor of the shack. The boy's parents struggled to believe the story. They thought somehow, the boy fell into the fishing hole and drowned. It was a tragedy, but alligators did not live in this part of the country, and no one would believe that a creature that size was living in the lake.

Only the boys knew. They saw it with their own eyes. But Don't be afraid, Pop-Pop has told this story before. Just Don't sneak out of your house at night, especially to go out to an ice shack. You Don't know what's under the ice!

5. The Ghost In The Closet

The boys were pretty sure that most of the closets in the house were safe. They each had a fear of what might be behind closet doors. So many of the doors were opened and closed throughout the day, so they got used to it.

The house was big, and there were a lot of rooms, and a lot of closet doors. The parents felt blessed to have four boys, even though it could be challenging at times. The two older boys shared a bedroom, and the twins each had their own crib in a room across the hall..

The parents bedroom was down the hall at the other end of the house. Sometimes it seemed their bedroom was miles away. Especially when they thought about that one closet door. The door that was never opened. Behind that door was a mystery. That door was so close to where they slept, and their parents bedroom was so far away.

The twins were too young to think about what might be behind that closet door, but the two older boys believed there was something scary on the other side. Sometimes they heard noises from behind the closet door. The twins saw how afraid their older brothers were, and wondered why. They started to imagine scary things in their own minds.

One night the older boy, Jack, woke up suddenly, thinking he heard something from the closet. Jack's reaction caused his younger brother Luke to wake up. Jack told Luke he heard something. They sat up in their beds and listened.

Sure enough, there was a whistling noise from across the hall. They heard the sound of a door opening, and then it shut. They were too afraid to run to their parents room, fearing that whatever it was would get them in the hallway.

They decided to call out loud to their parents. Mom & Dad came to the bedroom to see what was the matter. They checked out the closet and assured them everything was fine.

The next night when they went to bed, they closed the bedroom door, hoping to keep the noise from waking them up. Instead, the same thing happened. This time, they woke up to the sound of their own door opening. A cold misty cloud filled the room. They huddled up next to each other, and once again called for their parents. As they tried to scream out, their voices were silenced by the thick misty cloud. They could not cry for help.

An eerie voice cried out, "I'll be back tomorrow night. And after I get you, I'll go across the hall and get the twins. You will never rest while you live in this house, because I'll be back".

The misty cloud disappeared leaving Jack and Luke huddled together, afraid of what might happen next. They were afraid to move, and didn't speak a word. Finally they drifted off to sleep.

The next morning they each woke up in their own bed. Luke asked Jack if he remembered what happened. Jack said he had a bad dream, and told Luke the details. Luke told Jack that it couldn't have been a dream. How could they both have the same dream?.

On their way down to breakfast that morning, they passed the closet door across the hall. It was open. Jack pushed it shut. They looked at each other and thought the same thing. "That door wasn't open last night"!

Was it just a dream? They were sure it was not. But Don't be afraid. This is just another one of Pop-Pops stories. Or is it?

6. Princess and The Bull-Frog

It was the same thing every night. There was a large pond behind her house. It was time to go to sleep, but the bull frog that lived in the pond always kept the little girl awake. Every minute the bullfrog let out another echoing belch, like a dull foghorn.

Each morning, the little girl went out to the pond to see if she could find the bullfrog that made so much noise, keeping her awake at night. The pond was thick with weeds, and the water was muddy. She could never spot the bullfrog.

It was late in the summer, and the little girl had been playing with friends all day. She was tired, and wanted to fall asleep. The croak of the bullfrog was constant, and she thought it was getting louder. It was like the frog was right outside her window, belching away.

The next morning she told her Mother about the noise, and how it was keeping her awake. It was her only child, and she often referred to her little girl as Princess. She said to the little girl, "Don't worry my little Princess, I'll get you some earplugs to use at night so you Don't hear the frog"..

That night, the little girl put her earplugs in, hoping she could go to sleep without hearing the annoying bull-frog. It didn't work. Somehow, the noise grew even louder.

She went to the pond the next morning to see if she could find the frog. She hoped she could catch the frog and take him to another place to make the noise go away. Peeking out through the weeds, she saw two beady eyes, and a spotted green shiny nose staring up at her. She slowly reached down and snatched the frog out of the weeds with her hand.

She put the bull-frog in a jar, and showed her mother the culprit that was keeping her awake every night. The little girl's Mother agreed to drive to the other side of the pond to let the frog go. They drove to the far side of the pond and released the frog. "Now the frog can't bother you princess. It has a new home."

That night, the little girl went to her bedroom, looking forward to a quiet night, without the frog croaking away. The curtains were drawn. It was quiet and she started to drift off into sleep. But then, the echoing thunder of the belching frog returned, louder than ever. It sounded like the frog was right outside her window. She could not ignore it. She went to the window and pulled the curtains back.

What she saw made her jump back. She screamed. The head of the angry frog was as large as the window. The mean eyes were bright red surrounded by slimy green skin with foam oozing out the side of it's mouth. It no longer resembled a frog. Like a monster, it reared it's dragon-like head back and smashed it against the window.

Glass shattered and the head of the monstrous frog came right up to her face. She could smell his swampy breath, and tried to back away from the spray that was hitting her face.

The little girl was horrified. She screamed and covered her eyes. Then, as if her life depended on it, she remembered her Mother telling her the story of the Princess and the Frog. The Princess in the story kissed a frog and it turned into a Prince. She thought, "maybe if I kiss the frog, it will turn into a Prince."

But that story was a fairy tale. She pretended to kiss the frog, but it did not turn into a prince. You can only imagine what happened next. But you Don't need to worry. This is just Pop-Pops version of The Princess and the Frog.

7. The Bad Boy Farm

The fence was high, with barbed wire at the top to make it difficult for whoever was inside to escape. Behind the fence was a thick wall of trees that made it impossible to see the Bad Boy Farm. But the boys knew it was there. Jack and Luke had learned about it when they drove by with their Father one day. He told them all about it. It was a scary place, because that is where bad boys were sent.

Christmas had just passed, and Jack and Luke were happy that Santa had delivered them the gifts they wanted. They had heard all about Santa's rule that only good children got the presents they asked for. Santa was good to both of them that year. They got what they asked for. That was in spite of the fact sometimes they had both been bad. Bad to the point where they had been told Santa was not going to get them what they asked for.

Luke suggested to Jack that Santa must not really care about whether they were good or bad. Jack had to agree, because he got the train set he asked for. Luke added that he got the skateboard he had hoped for. But now they were learning about the Bad Boy Farm.

The Bad Boy Farm had been there for a long time. Pop-Pop had told their Father about it when he was a boy, and it was still the place they sent bad boys. So, they were very curious about what was inside the fence. They asked their Dad, "How bad do you have to be to get sent to the Bad Boy Farm"?

He told them what he knew. "When a Mom & Dad get frustrated because their boys are always misbehaving, they can call the Bad Boy Farm. At the farm, they promise to turn bad boys into good boys. If the boys turn into good boys, they can leave. If they Don't turn into good boys, they can't leave".

This is what their Father had heard…The building is old with no windows, so everything is dark. Once inside, there's a long hallway that leads to the rooms where the bad boys stay. There are no windows, and no lights. Each day, the bad boys get instructions from the Bad Boy Farm Instructor. They have to complete all of the instructor's assignments before the end of each day. The assignments include things like washing all of the floors with a mop and scrubbing down all of the walls with a scrub brush. They also have to be nice to the other boys, and the Instructor. Fighting or yelling will result in worse assignments, like scrubbing the toilets.

It was really quite simple. Learn to listen, behave and be nice. Once you have become a good boy, you can go home. That's what Jack and Luke's Father knew.

But there was more to it. If a bad boy does not learn to be good, he has to go to the basement.

At the end of the dark hall on the main floor, there is an elevator that goes to the basement. This is where the worst of the bad boys go. Some of them have been there for a long time. They are bigger and meaner. They bully the younger bad boys, and scare them at night.

But in the basement, the scariest thing is this...some of the Bad Boy Farm boys disappear, never to be seen again. They say that once you are in the basement with the worst of the bad boys, you are doomed. If you try to be good in the basement, the bad boys will get you! So, the best thing to do is avoid the Bad Boy Farm altogether.

This may or may not be one of Pop-Pops stories, but it might be better to play it safe. Just be a good boy, listen to your parents and be nice!

8. Groggies Pond

Jack & Luke had been looking forward to this night for a while. School was out, summer was here and the tent was set up in the backyard. It was a full moon tonight, and there were no clouds in the sky. Tonight was the first night the brothers were going to sleep outside in the tent. It would be just the two of them.

They crawled through the opening of the tent and rolled out their new sleeping bags. Jack made sure the opening of the sleeping bag was at the back end of the tent, away from the zippered door. Luke asked him why. Jack responded nervously, "In case somebody tries to get in." Luke agreed, but added, "Who would try to get in?"

Jack reminded him of the story Pop-Pop told them about the man called Groggie. Pop-Pop told them Goggie used to own the land their house was built on. He was a farmer with lots of land. In the middle of his farm there was a small pond.. Since it was on his land, they called it Groggies Pond. Groggie loved the pond. Whenever there was a full moon, he would venture down to see the reflection of the moon sparkling on the pond. He wanted the farm and the pond to last forever.

One day, Groggie was working on the fence that kept the cows from wandering away from his farm. One of the fence posts was rotted and needed to be replaced. Groggie had to use his circular saw to cut the new post down to the right size. While he was guiding the saw through the wood, it suddenly hit a Knot that caused the saw to snap back. Before Boggie could release the trigger, the blade hit his left arm, cutting into the bone. His arm could not be saved.

Without his left arm, he had trouble doing all of the work that needed to be done to keep the farm going. He decided to sell the farm to another farmer. He made the new farmer promise he would keep it as a farm. The new owner agreed, but years later he broke his promise. He sold his farm to a builder who built new homes all over the farm.

When Groggie found out, he swore he would get revenge. The only thing left of the farm was Groggies Pond. Whenever there was a full moon, the reflection still sparkled off the stillness of the pond. That's where Groggie decided to get his revenge.

One night, he walked through the neighborhood of new homes that had invaded his farm. The moon was full. Groggie was angry at what he was seeing. All of his beautiful land had been destroyed. He heard voices in the back yard of one of the homes. Quietly, Groggie walked behind the house, and saw a glow coming from inside a pitched tent. This would be his opportunity to take revenge. He approached the tent and waited for the noise to subside. There were two boys inside the tent. Once everything was quiet, he reached in with his right arm, the only arm he had, and grabbed one of the boys by the neck. The boy tried to scream, but he was being choked, and his voice was silenced. Groggie dragged him, struggling with his only arm around the boy's neck, and made his way to the pond.

The bright full moon was sparkling off the stillness of the pond. Did Groggie throw the boy in the pond? Was there a splash in the water that night? Who knows. The little boy was never found, and Groggie disappeared. Would Groggie reappear someday? Who knows.

Could this be another one of Pop-Pops stories? Who Knows?

9. The Graveyard

It was a long time ago. There were no school buses, and children had to walk down an old country road to get to the little one room schoolhouse. At the end of each day they walked back to their homes on the same country road.

As they sat in the classroom at the end of one school day, a heavy fog rolled in. It was time to walk home, but the fog was thick. The children could barely see the road in front of them. They stayed together and walked one in front of the other, making their way home.

Soon, they came to the graveyard. Many of their ancestors were buried there. It was never a big deal before, but now, the fog made the cemetery feel creepy. The children could barely make out the shapes of the eerie tombstones lined up in rows.

A narrow dirt road went through the center of the graveyard with tombstones on each side. One of the children dared any of the others to walk down the dirt road, past all of the tombstones. There was silence for a while. Finally, a little girl said to the others, "I'm not afraid. I'll walk to the end and back".

The children watched her disappear into the fog as she walked down the dirt road. They were waiting a long time when one of the children said, "she should have been back by now." The fog was getting thicker, and it was harder to see into the graveyard.

None of the kids wanted to go into the foggy graveyard to look for her, so they started yelling for her. There was no response. Finally they decided to walk down the dirt road together, looking for the little girl.

They called for her as they walked along. There was a faint voice in the distance. "I'm over here"! Her voice was weak and seemed to be drowned out by the thick fog.

The children stayed together, walking slowly toward the voice, but they could not find the little girl. She was lost in the graveyard.

The little girl was never found. The children still had to walk by the graveyard each school day. Every now and then the fog rolls in again. As the children walk by the graveyard they hear the faint sound of the lost girl pleading, "I'm over here"! They never stop to look for fear of being lost in the graveyard.

Pop-Pop has been to that graveyard, and says he thinks he heard the voice of the little girl. But is this another one of his stories?

10. Behind the Basement Wall

As much fun as it was to play in the basement, Jack and Luke never went down alone. All of their toys were down in the basement. They could kick the soccer ball around, set up obstacle courses, play games and beat on the drum-set without bothering their parents. But there was something scary about the basement.

One afternoon, their Mother called them up for dinner when they were in the middle of a game. Jack yelled up to his Mother, "Not yet we're playing a game". She called back down and told them they would need to finish the game later because dinner was ready. Luke yelled back, "Not yet, we're almost done". Of course, their Mother yelled back, "Now"!

Her command was followed by a few seconds of silence. Then, from behind the concrete wall, Jack & Luke heard a deep loud voice that echoed through the basement. The voice called out, "leave the basement now"!

Luke and Jack jumped up from their game and ran upstairs. They explained to their Mother that someone had called out to them from behind the wall. "Nonsense", she replied. Their Father agreed. "That's just your imagination", he told them. Jack responded, "but we both heard the voice"! The boys Mother snapped back, "Well if you would listen to me the first time, maybe that wouldn't happen".

They stayed away from the basement for a while, but one afternoon Jack and Luke were bored and wanted to play a game in the basement. They went down the stairs slowly, looking at all of the walls to make sure no-one was lurking around. After they were sure it was safe, they started playing a game. Once again, they were in the middle of a game when there Mother called them up for dinner. This time, they both jumped up and ran upstairs for dinner. Their parents were pleased that they had listened so well. Jack and Luke knew it was because they were afraid of the voice behind the wall. They never wanted to hear that voice again.

Pop-Pop says he has heard that voice in the basement. He says he was in the basement once, and a voice cried out, "This is not your basement"! Could it be?

11. Reese's Man

Jack had been craving a Reese's peanut butter cup ever since the last one he had from his halloween candy bag. His Mother promised she would get him one the next time they went to the store. When that day came, Jack was quick to remind his Mother. He directed her to the candy section of the store. The orange wrapper for the Reese's cup stood out among all the other candy. Jack wanted to grab one, but there was a man standing right in front of the box.

The man wore a long black leather coat and his eyes were hidden behind dark sunglasses. The top of his head was covered by a ratty knit hat with long straggly gray hair hanging down to his shoulders. His matching beard was a gnarly mess. He turned to Jack and his Mother and asked, "Looking for something?" Jack responded, "I just want to get a Reese's peanut butter cup." The man looked down at Jack and in his deep voice, mumbled, "fine, but you'll have to pay, because I am the Reese's man." Then he walked away and disappeared from the store.

Jack's Mother told him to ignore the man. They got the Reese's peanut butter cup and Jack couldn't wait to open it and take a bite. It was a treat, and he thanked his Mother.

The next day, Jack was kicking a ball around the back yard with his brothers. The ball bounced and rolled into a cluster of pine trees, and Jack chased it. When he got to the edge of the pine trees, the man from the store who called himself Reese's man suddenly appeared. "Where is my Reese's peanut butter cup? You must pay me now with a Reese's peanut butter cup." Jack was startled, and ran away from the man. He left the ball on the ground, somewhere in the cluster of pine trees.

Is the ball still there? Jack and his brothers are afraid to go look. Maybe they can get Pop Pop to go find the ball. Or maybe Reese's man is just Pop Pop in disguise.

12. Faker Man

Luke was having some fun riding his bike up and down the sidewalk in front of his house. He had been practicing to pedal and keep his balance without falling. After falling over and over again, he finally got the hang of it. He could ride one way down the sidewalk, turn around in the neighbors driveway, and pedal back up the sidewalk to his own driveway without falling.

One afternoon as Luke was riding back and forth on the sidewalk, a man approached. Luke had to stop his bike and let the man walk by him. As the man walked by he told Luke that he was impressed with how well he rode his bike, but added that he better be careful. That made Luke happy, and he peddled away with a smile..

The next day, Luke was riding his bike and the man reappeared. This time, the man was walking with a cane, like he had injured his leg. Luke noticed, and asked, "What happened to your leg?"

The man responded, "You ran over me with your bike." Luke was confused and responded, "No I didn't."

The man looked at him with glaring eyes and said, "Yes you did. I told you to be careful. When you go to sleep tonight, I'm going to sneak in and break your leg with my cane. Then you will know what it's like." The man limped away and disappeared out of sight.

Luke told his parents what happened with the man and his cane while they ate dinner. His Mother told him not to ride his bike anymore without supervision. His Father told Luke the man was probably faking his injury, but he had to stay away from him. He told Luke that if he ever saw this faker man again he was to let his parents know immediately.

That night, Luke was afraid to go to sleep, fearing the man would show up with his cane. It was a warm night and the windows were open to let fresh air in. The wind was blowing the curtains when Luke saw the man jump through the window, waving his cane. He was shouting at Luke, "I am not a faker man." He came closer to Luke and started to swing his cane down to hit Luke's leg. Luke tried to scream out, but his voice was not making a sound. Just before the cane reached his leg, the man vanished..

Was it a dream? Would Faker Man return? Luke will have to ask Pop Pop about that.

Printed in the USA
CPSIA information can be obtained
at www.ICGtesting.com
LVHW060606030424
776269LV00014B/215